This Little Tiger book belongs to:

_____

_____

_____

For my very best friend, Ann
- SS

Pour Billie Marilou, qui n'a pas peur des loups
— J D

LITTLE TIGER PRESS LTD,
an imprint of the Little Tiger Group
1 Coda Studios, 189 Munster Road, London SW6 6AW
www.littletiger.co.uk

First published in Great Britain 2019
This edition published 2019

Text copyright © Steve Smallman 2019
Illustrations copyright © Joëlle Dreidemy 2019
Steve Smallman and Joëlle Dreidemy have asserted their
rights to be identified as the author and illustrator of this
work under the Copyright, Designs and Patents Act, 1988

A CIP catalogue record for this book is
available from the British Library

All rights reserved · ISBN 978-1-78881-333-4
Printed in China · LTP/1400/2543/1118
10 9 8 7 6 5 4 3 2 1

THE WOLVES WHO CAME FOR DINNER

STEVE SMALLMAN   JOËLLE DREIDEMY

LITTLE TIGER
LONDON

Wolf and Hotpot were the very best of friends.

But the other animals who lived
in the forest were worried.

They just couldn't understand how
a wolf and a lamb could get along.

"Let's invite the bunnies for a playdate!"
suggested Wolf.
"Yippee!" cheered Hotpot.
So they spent all morning baking
carrot cupcakes.

But when Wolf opened the door
and said, "Teatime!" . . .
all the rabbits ran away!

Wolf sat down on the doorstep.
"But I'm not a bad wolf," he sighed. "I'm a GOOD wolf!"

"Good Woof!" agreed Hotpot. "Playtime now?"
"Yes!" cried Wolf. "And if the bunnies won't
come to us, we'll go to them!"

. . . Wolf couldn't understand why the only animal he found was Hotpot.

"Your friends are too good at hiding," sighed Wolf. "Looks like it's just you and me."

"Hop-Pop and Woof!" beamed Hotpot and gave him a big hug.

"I know!" cried Wolf. "We'll invite *my* friends over to meet *you*, Hotpot!"

But when Gripper, Nipper and Growler arrived they were starving.

"Yummy! We love hotpot!" they cried, licking their lips.

"Yes, well, I love Hotpot too!" said Wolf crossly. "And that's why you can't eat her! Now, how about some vegetable soup?"

Delicious!

After dinner
Wolf read them
a story.

Hotpot held
Gripper's hand
when it got to
the scary parts.

And by the end they
were all snuggled up
together, fast asleep.

But things didn't always go quite so well. Like the day Wolf and Hotpot were playing by the river. "Don't worry," said Wolf, holding Hotpot tightly. "I've got you!"

That wolf's got that lamb!

He'll gobble her up!

"Oh no!" the woodland creatures cried.
"We have to help her!"

Hotpot helped Wolf out of the water.
"Not paddling time, Woof, no!" she said. "Teatime!"
Wolf sighed and, taking Hotpot's paw,
he squelched sadly home.

But when they arrived, Gripper, Nipper and Growler were waiting by the door.

Oh no!

GASP!

More wolves!

"I told you," Wolf snapped. "You can't eat Hotpot!"

"We know!" called Gripper. "But could we have another story?"

"And a sleepover?" added Nipper and Growler. Wolf smiled and let them in.

And after more **delicious** soup,

silly stories,

and bedtime snuggles...

everyone fell *fast asleep*.

"We'll rush in on the count of three!" declared Fox. "One . . . two . . ."

The woodland creatures burst in but,

AWOO OOOO!

an eerie howl

stopped them in their tracks!

It was Hotpot!
    She gave the animals a hard stare
and said, "Not hurt my Woof, no!"

"Would it help if we ate some of them?" suggested Growler.

"No! Not hurt my friends!" answered Hotpot crossly.

Everyone looked a bit sheepish till Wolf said,

"How lovely to have so many visitors!

Sleepover, anyone?"

So everyone settled down in the
warm glow of the fire and
Wolf told them a story.

A story about making friends that was
funny, and exciting, and (a little bit) scary.
And at the end, like in most good stories,
they all lived happily ever after.

More super stories by Steve Smallman!

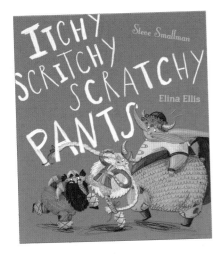

Itchy Scritchy Scratchy Pants
Steve Smallman
Elina Ellis

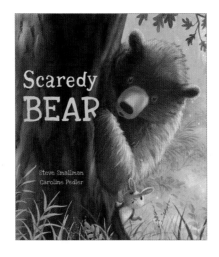

Scaredy BEAR
Steve Smallman
Caroline Pedler

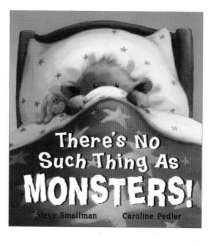

There's No Such Thing As MONSTERS!
Steve Smallman   Caroline Pedler

Don't Wake the Bear, Hare!
Steve Smallman
Caroline Pedler

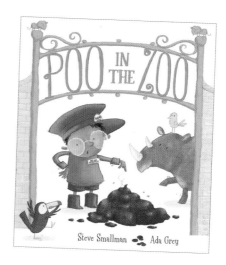

POO IN THE ZOO
Steve Smallman   Ada Grey

Bear's BIG Bottom
STEVE SMALLMAN & EMMA YARLETT

For information regarding any of the above titles or for our catalogue, please contact us:
Little Tiger Press, 1 Coda Studios, 189 Munster Road, London SW6 6AW
Tel: 020 7385 6333 · E-mail: contact@littletiger.co.uk · www.littletiger.co.uk